MARILYN AND MONET

Paul Levinson

Connected Editions

CONTENTS

1

Marilyn and Monty walked off the lot of *The Misfits* in the hot summer of 1960.

"There's a song in my head," she said to Monty, in that breathless voice that she sometimes used even off camera and stage.

"That stupid 'Teenie Weenie Yellow Polka Dot Bikini!'? That song's been driving me *crazy*," Monty said, with an exaggerated pout.

"No, something else." Marilyn laughed seductively. "About my being sexual," she explained, and pronounced the last word with an exaggerated British accent.

"Well, you *are*," Monty said. "So someone wrote a song about you? Who? Arthur?"

"No, not my husband," Marilyn said. "He hates me now."

Monty put a consoling arm on Marilyn's shoulder. "People find people they hate very sexy, all the time. Maybe even more," he said.

But you don't really find me sexy, Marilyn thought to herself about Montgomery Clift, *you don't react to me that way, and that's why I love you. I can really trust you.*

"But if not your husband, then who?" Monty asked. "You heard it on the radio? What's the name of the song?"

"No, not on the radio, in my head," Marilyn replied. "And I'm not sure about the name of the song."

"Hmmm," Monty said. "But you're sure it's about you?" he asked, teasingly. "I mean, not that you aren't the sexiest being in the known universe."

Marilyn squeezed his hand. "The beginning of the song is saying goodbye to me, by my real name, Norma Jeane."

***

Marilyn sipped Dom Perignon champagne in her room at the Mapes Hotel in Reno, Nevada and looked at the watercolor on the wall. It was by Monet, a common reproduction, she could tell, but it spoke to her, shimmering as if painted in tears, mirroring the tears so often on her face these days. She'd heard somewhere that some Frenchman had defined photography as rescuing images from their proper corruption in time. If that was true, then it seemed to her that Impressionistic paintings like this Monet did just the opposite, pulling her right through time and its corruptions. She certainly felt corrupted now, more than ever before, and that was a fact.

There was a knock on her door. It was Peter Lawford. She hugged him. He felt so thin, like a leaf quivering in her arms. He was well cast in *The Thin Man* on television. Or maybe she was the one who was quivering.

He smiled at her -- that rich, incandescent smile -- and offered his hand. "Come," he said, in his British baritone, "there's someone who wants to see you."

"Who?" Marilyn asked, coyly, though she thought she knew exactly who.

"You'll see," Lawford answered with equal coyness.

They drove in Lawford's car to the local bar. Elvis's "Don't" was playing on the jukebox. Marilyn was aware of her body swaying, almost of its own volition, to the sensual strains of Elvis's voice.

Lawford gestured to a table at the far side of the room. Marilyn was surprised. Seated at the table was one man, even thinner than Lawford, and, unlike the suave actor, as nervous as hell. Not the man she had expected -- his brother.

The music suddenly changed -- whether on the jukebox or just in her head, Marilyn couldn't be sure. It was that singer who had made the record, "Teenager in Love" -- Marilyn loved that, she always felt like a teenager when she was in love, which was just about always, with one man or another. But the voice wasn't singing that song. It was something much more heart-rending, about looking for Bobby -- the man who was seated at the table she and Lawford were now approaching.

Bobby stood as Marilyn approached, took her hand, and asked her to dance. They'd met a few months earlier, but this was the first time he'd asked Marilyn to dance. Lawford smiled, took a seat, and summoned the waiter for more alcohol.

Bobby and Marilyn danced slowly to the music. She heard that same song in her head, over and over again. It almost sounded like a dirge. The song mentioned Abraham, then Martin, then John, then Bobby. She knew no one named Abraham or Martin, yet she felt as if she should.

She wondered if Bobby was hearing the same song. If not, what was he dancing to?

He ran his hand down her back. It felt good, a lot like his brother John's. They swayed to the music, but the song was starting to make her crazy. "Do you hear that?" she finally asked Bobby, softly, in his ear.

"What, the song?"

"Yes," she answered. "It's strange."

"It's a new version of 'Over the Rainbow'," Bobby said. "I find the harmony quite evocative."

"Yes," Marilyn said, and what she had been hearing seemed to melt into "Over the Rainbow," which had words about something melting, as Marilyn's face melted into tears, which she hoped would be absorbed without notice into the blue cotton shirt on Bobby's shoulder.

She looked over Bobby's shoulder at a glass of rosé on an unoccupied table. They were indoors, but she could see the sun setting in the glass.

***

She awoke the next morning with a throbbing headache and a world of misgivings. She looked again at the Monet above the table. It had captured light from a lovely day that no longer existed. Was her brain somehow an antenna that captured music from bad days which didn't exist yet at all?

Arthur her husband might know, even though she was sure that he soon would no longer be her mate. She laughed to herself sarcastically about the term. Arthur had never been her soulmate, as that poet, maybe Coleridge -- she had read him in high school long ago -- had put it. No, Joe was her soulmate and would always be. But Arthur had the brains. He was the smartest man she had ever known. If anyone could understand what was going on in her brain, Arthur Miller would.

There was a phone on her night table by the bed, and another phone on the dresser across the room. She thought about calling Arthur from her bed. Normally she liked talking to men this way, especially in the nude, but she didn't feel like that today.

She rose, walked by the window, and looked at herself in the long mirror on the wall. The sunlight seeping through the curtains worked well against her body. She smiled. She had something of the director in her. Someday she would like to direct a movie, if this insane life of hers ever gave her the time.

She enjoyed the sight of her body in the mirror. However disordered her brain might now be, her body was still fine. She sat by the phone and wished that there were picture telephones already, like the ones she had heard they were working on at Bell Labs. She'd love to call Arthur and have him see her like this. He'd like that. Or maybe not. You never knew with him.

She rose again, put on a negligee, sat back down by the phone and called him.

"Hello," Arthur Miller said.

His voice sounded good. "It's me," Marilyn said, sounding a bit more like a little girl than she'd intended.

"Oh hello," Arthur said again. "I was just thinking about you."

Ordinarily that would have been welcome, but something in the tone of his voice said otherwise. "I wanted to talk to you about something," Marilyn said.

"Me too," Arthur said. "Why don't you go first."

"No, you," Marilyn said.

Arthur took a slow breath. "I've been thinking we should stop prolonging the agony and end our marriage. Don't you?"

***

The songs about death in her head seemed to subside after that, maybe because the barbiturates she increasingly dosed herself with to go to sleep had shut down that part of her brain. But she needed those pills. They gave her precious time. She liked the fact that her make-up could be put on when she was still sound asleep on drugs in the morning. She usually remembered to put on a negligee before she went to sleep, but enjoyed thinking about people looking at her when she was in dreamland, having their own dreams about her.

Clark died shortly after *The Misfits* was finished. She'd had no premonitions, heard no songs in her head, about that. Maybe because her world had changed. Arthur was gone. Joe got her out of the loony hospital, and they were friends again. All seemed to be going tolerably well, until--

That night of the President's birthday celebration at Madison Square Garden in May 1962. She had on the perfect dress - sheer and shimmering with thousands of rhinestones, reflecting and refracting her light, a soft and seductive second flesh, riding on hers. She had worked out a little shtick with Peter. He would introduce her several times during the ceremony, but she would wait until just the right time to appear on stage. All to ratchet up the excitement.

She carefully kept track of the number of faux introductions. Ok, she was set to walk out on stage after the next one. Peter introduced her as "the late Marilyn Monroe".

The audience laughed and applauded. She assumed the President was laughing, too. But the adlib shattered her -- it wasn't part of the routine. The word "late" clanged loudly in her head and seemed to confirm all the premonitions she had been having about her mortality the past few years, and now about the President and his brother, too.

She had intended to sing "Happy Birthday, Mr. President" with a quick tempo and a zest, but she walked up to the microphone, took in the applause, and delivered her song like a zombie.

2

C laude Monet looked at his dear wife Camille on her sickbed. Her face was whiter than the sheets, stripped of their color by the tuberculosis which now combined with other ailments to daily sap her of her young life. In the blizzard of pale that confronted him, he thought of his countryman Louis Pasteur, and all the marvels of medicine he had perfected. But no cure for his wife was yet among them, and now her time would soon be at an end. With all the many wonders of this great 19th century, it still had a ways to go in conquering the many age-old enemies of humanity.

He thought about color, which was always in his mind in one way or another. Life was color. Death was its absence. And lack of all color was not to be mistaken for an appealing whiteness in living skin tone. His friend Renoir had captured that beautifully in his nudes. Monet had never attempted to paint a nude. Not out of respect for his wife, as some had suggested. Not because of some moral prohibition -- to the contrary, Monet thought that the road to immorality resided in not following one's artistic vision.

No, Monet had never painted a nude, because, as best as he could tell from the many models he had seen unclothed in the galleries of friends, none had the subtle texture of color that he craved for his paintings. The closest he had seen was his friend Pierre Renoir's evocative "Nude in the Sun," finished just three years ago, in 1876, the same year in which Camille had first become ill with tuberculosis. There was something about the face and expression in that painting -- ironically, not the body -- which spoke to Monet, seemed to reach out to him from some blurry eternity. The model, Anna LeBoeuf, just 20 years of age and Renoir's mistress, was more appealing, more special, to Monet's eyes than was Renoir's previous beauty, also his mistress, Lise Tréhot. It was also not missed by Monet that Anna's very surname, LeBoeuf, spoke of nudity in American slang, in the buff. Something also told him that Lisa's last name had a sensual connotation in some language, but he wasn't sure of that.

***

For some reason, Monet thought about Anna a lot in the months that followed, and he decided to go see her. He was sure Renoir would not mind. The two men had literally sat side by side, and painted the same scene, and Monet was pretty sure that the reason he wanted to see Anna was not because he wanted to paint her or bed her. He just wanted to see her ... in the nude.

He met her at the cafe. She was not naked, but was wearing a soft lilac dress that made it easy for him to imagine how she would look with no clothes. She was sipping wine and reading a book of poetry -- *Les Fleurs du Mal* by Charles Baudelaire. The late afternoon sun played with the ringlets of her hair. Monet noticed immediately that her curls were darker than they appeared in Renoir's painting. He smiled. He knew that he and no painter was immune to taking liberties with the hues of people and things captured on canvas, especially when it came to imbuing them with more sunlight.

He took her hand and kissed it.

She smiled at him with her rose petal lips. "I'm a great admirer of your work," she said.

"Thank you," he replied and took a seat. "And I of yours."

A waiter approached with a glass of Bordeaux for Monet. Anna was sipping something lighter.

"You came here to talk about putting me in one of your pictures?" Anna asked, still smiling. "Pierre would have no objection."

Monet tasted his wine and nodded his approval to the waiter, who bowed and left.

"I like getting right to the point," Anna added, with an even bigger smile.

"I do, as well," Monet replied and returned the smile. "But, no, painting your portrait is not exactly what I would like to do with you."

She looked at him quizzically, with a different kind of smile. "You really do like getting to the point, don't you." And she laughed, and it sounded like summer rain.

Monet laughed a little, too. "No, not that either," he said. "And, actually, painting you may not be that far away from what I would like to do with you."

"Now I'm confused," Anna said, and regarded Monet even more quizzically.

Monet sipped his wine and looked at her. "I'd like to see you in the nude, with an eye towards deciding if I might want to paint you that way."

Anna opened her mouth but said nothing.

"I hope you do not find that prospect insulting," Monet said.

"Auditioning me to be your model for a nude painting?" Anna replied. "No, I'm am nothing but flattered at the prospect, and its potential for making me immortal as one of your subjects."

"I'll pay you--"

"Absolutely not," Anna said, and wagged a flirtatious finger at Monet. "I don't take money from such good friends of good friends."

"Thank you," Monet said and sighed in relief. "When can I come see you?"

"I have all sorts of unbreakable appointments this month," Anna replied. "How about two weeks from Tuesday -- would the morning light suit you?"

"Indeed it would."

***

Monet got the news three days before that appointed Tuesday. Anna had been felled by a sudden attack of smallpox, and had died.

He found it hard to paint anything, let alone a nude, in the excruciating months ahead. Anna's death seemed a rebuke to him -- as if the cosmos was saying no to what he had intended to do with her. The universe was telling him -- you exceeded your bounds -- no one, not even you, can capture that kind of beauty on canvas.

Camille's condition worsened, too.

Her soul finally left her, in September. She was just 32. Monet painted her lifeless face. The tears in his eyes gave the watercolor a texture he had never seen before.

Monet stared at the portrait and considered. Death had now robbed him twice. First of the nude he had never painted, now of his sweet wife. Painting was supposed to be about the immortal. But everything Monet had touched or wanted to touch seemed to turn into fleeting ashes, like the thinnest of paper in flame.

3

Marilyn walked along the beach in Contra Costa, California, and gazed at the quiet Pacific. The July colors were especially pastel and beautiful, like most of the sunsets in this part of the world. She was thinking about the tequila she had sipped not long ago with Emilio Fernández -- "El Indio" -- her moustachioed Mexican director. Something about this sunset and its colors spoke tequila to her. She even heard a song in her head about tequila, but she wasn't sure if it was about just another sunset or sunrise, and was glad it wasn't about her death.

She thought about walking here naked and jumping into the ocean, like she had in that swimming pool scene in *Something's Gotta Give*. She thought about swimming out as far as she could, until she passed out from sweet exhaustion and tequila, and her body washed up slick and nude and tempting on a beach somewhere. Imagine the press a discovery like that would generate! Marilyn in the morning had walked out to sea ...

She looked at the last of the sunlight, and the sparkling necklace it made on the water. It was a necklace fit for a princess. Suddenly, unbidden, that Goodbye Norma Jeane song began playing off the water. Except the lyrics were somehow different -- they were about a fallen princess named England's Rose. What did this mean? Marilyn had once been in a movie about a prince, with Olivier, but she had played a showgirl not a princess. She cleared her head and the music stopped and she wasn't sure if she actually had heard that song or she was now just remembering an illusion.

She kicked off her sandals and put a tentative foot in the warm water. It felt good, comforting, but she didn't take her clothes off. She didn't jump in. She didn't want to die. She looked at the mauve colors, literally watercolors in the water. She didn't especially believe in life after death, and wanted to be alive, to continue taking in these lavenders, baby pinks, and azure blues.

She walked a little further on the shore and sat on a big rock. Its moss made a convenient cushion. She had a transistor radio in her purse and she felt like turning it on but knew it wouldn't be playing the music she wanted to hear, very different from what had just been playing in her head on the water. You didn't hear that old music very often any more, not since she'd been a doe-eyed girl two decades ago.

She played the music on her turntable mind instead, this time deliberately, as she looked out at the rippling mirrors of water. Where had it gone? Glenn Miller's "In the Mood"? It was all rock 'n' roll now.

Where had Glenn Miller gone, disappearing like that in that plane over the English Channel near the end of the war? Where had that girl named Norma Jean gone? She was not here on this shoreline anymore.

She impulsively turned on her radio. She realized that there was a song she wanted and thought she had a chance of hearing -- Acker Bilk's "Stranger on the Shore". But it wasn't playing, either.

She played that mournful clarinet in her imagination, instead. She could hear Acker Bilk's tongue, wet on the woodwind reed, she could feel it on her ear. She saw a rocket ship sail straight up to the moon, but there was no moon outside now, it was morning, and she didn't know what she was seeing. She was Marilyn in the mourning.

***

Marilyn returned to her Brentwood home and stretched out on her bed. She felt the way she always did these days, oddly invigorated but exhausted, at the same time. She realized she still hadn't recovered from those four days the year before in a padded cell in the Payne Institute, very literally a pain, not only in her posterior but her soul.

Everything was wrong about that, every doctor wanting to be helpful, every nurse, but only making things worse. Except that nice young surgeon, Leonard Shlain, who had come to see a friend, another doctor, but had stopped when he walked by Marilyn's room, which the orderly had accidently left with the door ajar.

Dr. Shlain immediately recognized her, and had apologized for the intrusion as he walked into her room. He spoke to her of goddesses in mythology, and reviews of her movies in the newspapers, of time and space in science and art, of Einstein and Monet, and although she could barely understand him, what he said made a strange kind of sense to her, and she was flattered by the conversation. He mentioned at some point that he was attached to Bellevue -- good thing he hadn't told her that when he'd first walked in, she likely would have told him to leave if he'd said that. It has bad enough she was here at Payne, she didn't want to be associated with that Bellevue lunatic asylum in any manner, shape, or form. Yeah, the papers would have had a bloody field day with that story, too!

Shlain concluded the conversation, apologized again for the intrusion, and left, closing the door behind him. She had known, for some reason, that she'd never see this doctor again--

Her phone rang in her Brentwood bedroom, ending her recollection. She smiled when she heard the voice. It was Joe, one of her last true friends in this world.

4

Monet knew that time and light were intimately interconnected. What he tried to do in his painting was capture the light as it fled through time. Photographers, Daguerre and his offspring, captured the object or the scene as light bounced off it and registered on the photographic plate. But Monet, Renoir, and their friends tried to capture the light itself in transit.

Monet sometimes thought about the larger implications of what they were doing. If he was fixing light itself on his canvas, was he also capturing time? And what could he do with that time on his hands? He smiled at his own wordplay.

It was now 1899, the eve of the new millennium, nearly a quarter century after Anna and then Camille had left this Earth, but he thought of them many times a day, much as he dearly loved his Alice. Camille and Anna somehow fed his growing obsession with time. To express that, he had for several years now taken to painting the same exact scene at different times of day. This seemed to him the clearest way of capturing time itself. If the physical object was the same, all that remained to distinguish one of his paintings from the others was the passage of time itself.

He had recently read a scientific romance novel by H. G. Wells. Monet could neither read nor even speak English, but he had an enormous affection for the culture and the people ever since he had taken refuge on the island to avoid the war between his country and Prussia in 1871. Mercure de France had been good enough to bring out a French translation of *The Time Machine*, and Monet had devoured every page of it.

He had read some of the fanciful novels of his countryman, Jules Verne, but they lacked the profundity of this work by Wells, which spoke to the very thoughts that had been intriguing and bedeviling him: could time itself be manipulated such that one could use it to travel from one time to another in the same way that living things and objects quite naturally traveled from one place to another, unless they were affixed by roots to the ground, as was a plant with flowers which had not yet been picked, or an edifice of brick which was impossible to move intact.

He had been thinking of somehow capturing that force of time in his paintings of light. Wells had used a machine, a carriage drawn not by a horse but by time. Paintings and carriages, whether horsedrawn or horseless, had little in common -- but was there some common ground nonetheless between him and Wells worth exploring?

He looked out at his floating garden in Giverny and the lilies he was painting -- white, yellow, and blue lilies and their reflections, which reddened with time in the very pigment of the delicate petals like a sun going down in a sky over water. He imagined walking into one of his paintings and sitting on a lily of time -- wide enough to support his bottom -- and being instantly transported to the times this lily would gradually inhabit as it pinkened.

Yes, he needed to talk to Wells about the pink of time and how it might be harnessed. He had no plans to travel to England now -- he was far too comfortable here in his garden -- and he had no idea if the author of *The Time Machine* was in France or was scheduled to be.

Monet reached for the pen, ink, and paper that were never far from his easel. He would write a letter to Wells, in his favorite blue-violet ink, and trust in their mutual friends at Mercure to get the correspondence to the English author.

***

Wells was perfecting a chapter in his novel, *When The Sleeper Awakes*, in his study in Sandgate when his wife Jane arrived with the letter from Claude Monet. It was actually two letters, one written by Monet, the other a translation into English by an unknown clerk working at the Mercure de France in Paris. Wells was familiar with the publisher, and enjoyed the poetry it had brought out by Stéphane Mallarmé, which Wells had read in translation.

"I've always loved Monet's work," Jane said, putting her hand affectionately on her husband's shoulder. "He could have been a botanist, had he not become a painter. His depictions of flowers show something unique of their essence, something that evades even the truest photographs."

Wells took her hand and kissed it. "High praise, coming from someone who studied in my biology laboratory." He liked thinking about and reminding her of the place they first had met and fallen in love, just seven years ago, in the University Tutorial College in London.

Jane stroked her husband's face. "What does he say?" she asked him, about Monet's letter.

"You haven't read it yet yourself?" Wells replied with a smile.

Jane returned the smile. "I have, but I wanted your interpretation."

Wells read the translation aloud. "He's wondering if time travel could be possible through the light he paints on his canvas," Wells said, and slowly shook his head no.

"You don't believe it is?" Jane asked.

"I'm not sure it is in any case, whether through light itself or via a machine that someone invented as in my book," Wells replied.

Jane considered.

Wells frowned. "This is possible," he said, holding up the chapter from the new book he was writing. "Someone lapses into a coma and wakes up in a new world 200 years later. That violates no natural law. But travel through time? I don't think so. Still, I'm honored he asked me."

"What are you going to say to him?" Jane asked.

Wells shook his head again. "I need to think about that."

Jane smiled knowingly. "You find something in Monet's idea of interest, am I right?"

"Perhaps."

"You've worked light and its properties, and our capacity to manipulate them, into *The Invisible Man*," Jane said, "maybe you and Monet are not too far away in your thinking." She gestured to the red book with gold-embossed printing on the shelf overhead.

"That's your favorite of the books I've written, I know," Wells said, then stood up to take *The Invisible Man* from the shelf. He also helped himself to a copy of *The Time Machine*, in dark beige binding.

"Not true," Jane said, mischievously. "Every book you've written is my favorite."

***

Alice strode briskly up to Monet in his garden. She knew better than to interrupt him when he was painting, but he was reading a book now -- it looked like Flaubert's novel, *Salammbô*, a story about Carthage three centuries before Christ, which for some reason her husband was reading now -- and he usually didn't complain if she talked to him when he was reading.

"Yes?" he looked up from his book with a smile.

"It's a letter from H. G. Wells, and a translation from Mercure," Alice said, and handed the papers to Monet. "A reply to the letter you sent to him?"

Monet eagerly took the letters and raced through them. "Yes," he finally said, "it is his reply."

"And what does he tell you? Does he agree with you that travel through time in an instant is a possibility?"

"No," Monet said slowly. "He does not."

"Oh ..." But Alice thought that the English author must have written something helpful in his letter, otherwise her husband would have been cross.

"He does not think actual, physical travel through time is possible," Monet explained, "other than by just living through it. But he believes light may be a conduit of time."

Alice struggled to understand. "But when you painted your lilies yesterday, and we look at the painting today, have you not fixed the light of the lilies so we can see today exactly what they looked like yesterday? And was not that mirror of the past already known to you?"

Monet nodded, impressed as he often was with her quick and deep intelligence. "That is light from yesterday, visible to us today, therein giving us a window onto the past. Monsieur Wells is talking about just the opposite."

Alice furrowed her brow. "I don't see--"

"Wells thinks -- just as a theoretical possibility, but nonetheless -- that it might be possible to refract some light from the future back to the present."

"How?" Alice asked.

"This is just speculation," Monet said, "but Wells thinks the way that such light could be refracted and reflected back to us could be via a mechanism or process yet to be invented -- in the future."

"When will that happen? We have nothing at all like that reverse photography or painting now."

"I know," Monet said. "I don't care about cameras and photographs. As for my painting ... Wells says I just have to wait, and images from the future might one day come to me." He turned from Alice to the lilies in his garden and resumed his brushwork on a canvas he had touched a few hours earlier.

5

Marilyn awoke as if in a gauze and rubbed the sleep from her eyes. She had been having that dream again, the one that had been coming to her often in these hot California summer days. The pills were no doubt to blame, she was sure. But she needed the pills to sleep, and the dream was attractive as well as disconcerting.

She was sleeping under lush covers in the nude. An old man, no one she recognized, was in the room, and he gently pulled off the covers. He unwrapped her, as he might a precious package. He looked at her body, with pleasure in his eyes, but in a way that was not quite lascivious. He had an unkempt, straggly beard, off-white and dirty grey, too long in the front. He almost looked like a derelict, but his eyes said otherwise, and had a luminous intensity and wisdom that stirred Marilyn deeply in her drugged sleep.

She came more fully awake and put the dream aside. She toyed with going back to sleep in the hope of resuming the dream, but she had a meeting this morning with Darryl. Fox had wisely brought him back after firing that inexperienced jackass Levathes, who had given her so much trouble. She rose from the bed and put on her bathrobe. Just thinking about what Levathes had done to her -- firing her for no good reason, suing her for breath of contract, hiring that goodie two-shoes Lee Remick to take her place -- was more than enough to get Marilyn fully awake and fired up. Good thing Dino, God bless him, had been a mentch and refused to work with Remick. Marilyn was sure Darryl Zanuck would take her back and they'd finish the movie.

It was an idiotic comedy about a photographer -- Marilyn's role -- who disappears in the Pacific and is declared legally dead. She returns after five years and the damn family dog is the only one who remembers her! Well, she was a fan of comedies, and knew they had their place, and besides, *Something's Gotta Give* seemed to have a real pertinence to her life. The part about being dead, which was never too far from her mind these days.

***

Darryl was good enough to send a limo to pick her up for their meeting. The driver was a handsome, energetic young Negro, who reminded her of Jackie Robinson.

"Would you care to listen to some music along the ride?" he asked her, after he seated her comfortably and provided the tequila paloma she had requested.

"Why yes," Marilyn said, breathlessly. "Classical would be wonderful."

"Of course," the driver said, and turned on the radio. Debussy's "Afternoon of a Faun" came on, someplace near the beginning.

Marilyn sipped her drink, closed her eyes, and enjoyed the clarinets. She soon realized she was listening to another song, something about Jackie Robinson, no it was about his wife ... and then she realized the words were not about just about Mrs. Robinson, either, but about her own husband, Joe DiMaggio. She'd always loved that Les Brown song about her husband, but this song was something different, about a lonely nation. Like some of the other strange songs that had come to her in the past few years, she felt there was something not right about this, or something she shouldn't be hearing ...

"Ma'am," the driver voice interrupted her reveries. She opened her eyes and realized she had dozed off a little, and they were now in front on the Fox studio office.

"Thank you," she said, as the driver helped out her seat. She favored him with a big smile and proceeded to her meeting with Darryl Zanuck.

6

Alice had another letter from H. G. Wells in her hand. She felt it was safe to interrupt her husband. He was in the garden, but he wasn't painting. He was listening, with eyes half closed, to a phonograph recording of "Prélude à l'après-midi d'un faune" on the new Berliner Gramophone she had bought him last month as a present for no reason. Claude loved everything by his good friend also named Claude, especially this soft, moody composition, which he thought was the very embodiment in breathless sound of the light he sought to capture in his paintings, and based on a poem by Stéphane Mallarmé, whom Monet also loved, and thought his words also captured that same ineffable spirit of their age.

Monet lowered the volume to the level made by a quiet brook, and took the letter and translation from Alice. He read through it several times, and smiled ironically.

"What does he say?" Alice finally asked.

"He thinks it may be possible that some few people may exist across many times, or at least a part of them."

"But that's good for what you want, no?" Anna asked.

"Yes and no," Monet replied. "Wells cautions me several times that this is just speculation on his part, just fiction, and not natural science. And then he says he is thinking of writing one of his stories about this, and asks if he could have my permission."

"What will you tell him?"

"I don't know," Monet said, "I'd like to somehow make this not fiction but real -- that's after all what all of my painting is about."

7

Marilyn came home from the meeting feeling invigorated, more optimistic and alive than she'd felt in months, maybe years! Darryl was a complete gentleman -- he definitely wanted to rehire her for *Something's Gotta Give* and also star in another movie, *What a Way to Go*! Let Lee Remick make another murder movie.

Marilyn couldn't wait to get to the phone in her home and share the good news. She tried Joe -- no answer. She tried Frank -- no answer, either. Jesus, why didn't these guys get one of those new telephone-recording machines? She laughed -- she hadn't yet bothered to get one of those herself yet, either.

She called her shrink.

"Dr. Ralph Greenson's office," that secretary with the ridiculous sing-song California accent answered the phone.

Marilyn was quickly connected to Greenson, and told him what happened. "I'm so excited!" she concluded, "I feel like everything's gonna come up roses from now on!"

"That's wonderful," Greenson said, reassuringly. "But remember what we've been discussing. You don't want to get too high, and you don't want to get too low. Right in the middle, on a nice, even keel, is where we want you to be."

"Ok," Marilyn said, uncertainly. She hadn't really called Greenson for reassurance. More for celebration.

"I can give you more medication, to keep you calm and relaxed, when you come see me this afternoon," Greenson said.

"Ok," Marilyn said, "if that what's you think is best." She got off the phone. But she wasn't sure if Greenson's prescription was really for the best now. She loved feeling alive, flying, really wanted, adored by her public. And Darryl was giving her a chance to get there again.

Why did these shrinks always throw cold water on your best days? She supposed Greenson was preferable to that witch doctor, Dr. Marianne Kris, who had committed her to Payne.

Though she had thought very highly of Kris before Payne. In fact, she still loved her, in a way. Marilyn had had a great conversation with her about that recently published book *Art and Illusion*, written by a Kris family friend, another Austrian guy by the name of Gombrich. The book had been on Kris's desk. Its idea had been that great works of art didn't just appear on the canvas overnight -- no, painters had to work at it, years sometimes, trying this and that, trial and error, until they got it right. That was the essence of Strasberg's method, which Marilyn adored, and Gombrich had said that was the way Manet and Monet, the two great painters with almost the same name, had worked. Painting the same thing, the same scene, over and over, and until they got it just right.

She thought about one of her favorite Monet paintings -- "Sunrise". He had gotten that sun just right, too. She recalled that Yves, her French lover, had also loved that painting. That's what she was feeling now. She was the sun rising out of a murky sea, brightly shining forever.

***

Marilyn took a nap in a chair, and dreamed something that was in many ways stranger than what she had been hearing in her head these past few years. She did hear a song -- one which she couldn't recognize -- with unusual music, and words about holes and a place called Albert Hall. Wait -- yes -- she thought maybe she knew that place, the Royal Albert Hall in South Kensington, right? But that wasn't what was so strange about this dream. It was the bizarre LP album cover, which contained the record she was sure was the source of the music. The cover had four rows of a huge number people standing crowded together. Mae West and Huntz Hall were among those on the top row. Tony Curtis, Oliver Hardy, and H. G. Wells -- she loved his novels -- were on the second row. And -- oh my God -- she herself was also on that row, looking pretty svelte in a gold dress! She was sure she had never seen this before. And a part of her asked, where did it come from? And another part said, it hasn't been released yet. But, then, how did she know about this? And what did it mean that she was on this cover? Some of the people, like poor Oliver Hardy, were dead. Others, like cute Tony Curtis, were very much alive. She listened to the music more carefully. Maybe that would have an answer. But it was growing stranger, something about turning on--

She awoke with a start. She changed into a more comfortable cotton dress, and decided to put in a call to her third shrink, Margaret Hohenberg. She needed an interpretation of this crazy dream. She had an embarrassment of psychiatric riches -- three of them mixing up her mind. She hadn't seen Margaret for an in-person session in years, but she still enjoyed talking to her on the phone.

Margaret greeted her warmly.

"I want to talk to you about a dream I just had," Marilyn said.

"My specialty," Margaret said.

Marilyn told her about the album cover, and identified as many people as she could recall. "I think Karl Marx was also there," she concluded.

Margaret chuckled. "Maybe you're a secret Communist," she said. "But not to worry, that Black List is over, yes?"

"Yeah," Marilyn said, not finding that particularly funny. "And you're not allowed to talk about what we talk about, right?"

"Yes, of course," Margaret replied. "Was there any writing you could make out on the cover? The name of the recording artist, perhaps?"

Marilyn concentrated. "Maybe," she finally said. "Maybe - beetles -- and don't tell me I'm buggy!" Now she laughed, too.

Margaret joined in. "Sense of humor is a sure sign of sanity," she eventually said.

Again, reassurance Marilyn didn't want. Because, she would bet her very life on the fact that what she was seeing in her dreams and hearing in her head was real and true -- far more so than the movies she was fighting so hard to be a star of. But she also knew that no one, shrink or studio head, would ever believe her.

8

Wells sat in his study in his Sandgate home, glad for the warmth of the crackling fire in his hearth. It was a new year -- January, 1926 -- and something very important had just happened with his correspondent Monet, with whom he had been discussing time travel for years.

Wells held in his hand the latest communication from Monet, received just an hour ago. Monet was asking Wells to burn all of their correspondence, saying it was just about a fantasy that had no place in the historical record. Monet was 86 years old -- 26 years older than Wells -- and had been saying in his last few letters that he felt he hadn't much time left on this Earth, and wanted to see to it that history remembered him well.

Wells understood that. Even at 60, he was very much aware of his own mortality. Poor health had driven him here to Sandgate at the turn of the century. But he found that he couldn't agree with Monet.

First, even if Wells consigned to the fire all of the letters he had received from Monet over the years, and the painter did the same with those he had received from Wells, there were still the people who had translated the correspondence at the French Mercury. What guarantee could either he or Monet have that the translators had not written out their own copies, like the scribes of the Middle Ages? After all, he and Monet were both inordinately famous, in their own ways.

But there was something else, an idea that recently had popped into his head, which Wells had confided as yet to no one, including Monet. It was a straightforward, if utterly insane, idea. What if the mere thinking and writing about something could make it so in the world? In a sense, this was the ultimate premise of all of his scientific fiction stories -- of everyone's fiction about science. Verne had written about a flight to the moon. That had not happened as yet. But were not the aircraft which flew in the Great War a big step towards what Verne was writing about, and which didn't exist yet at the time of Verne's writing?

Wells proposed to himself that he would write a story about Monet, in which the painter's thoughts about capturing lights and images from the future became a reality.

***

Monet was grateful for his sight, which itself seemed almost a miracle to him now. The operations to remove the cataracts that occluded his eyes had gone well. Indeed, he was now sure he could see certain hues and shades of color he had not been able to see before, at any time in his life. He was beginning to see other things more clearly, too.

He looked out at his garden. It was June 1, and the water was never more alluring. He felt something beautiful had come into the world this day, and as he took in his lilies in the water he realized that this beauty he was sensing came from someplace much further away.

He glanced down at the correspondence he had received this morning. Still no response from Wells, no reply to the letter he had sent the writer nearly six months earlier, in January.

He coughed. His chest hurt. Everything hurt these days, except his eyes. He had seen so much death in the Great War, and had painted weeping willows as his homage. He felt his own death could not be far away. But just as people die, other people are born, and that was a consolation. He wondered, in this year of 1926, who of note would be born to replace him?

He saw water in his reverie -- not the still water of his lily pond, but waves of rolling water on some distant shore. A woman was walking along it, her shoeless feet in the water. Beautiful blonde hair, diaphanous dress, slightly blowing in the soft sea breeze, and she seemed to be looking at him.

My God, she was an angel. Even at his age, Monet loved looking at her body, the curves of her breasts and her thighs, lily white against the curves of the turquoise waves. He was attracted to curves, as both a painter and a man. He was half awake, and knew he wanted to paint what he was seeing. But how? The memory in his mind's eye was not as strong as it used to be. He had the will, and he believed the talent, but not the biological apparatus he had when he was younger. If he wanted to paint this voluptuous beauty, he would have to see her in person, literally in the flesh, walking upon this shore.

But he had no idea where she was. And then he realized he had no idea when this was, though a part of him suspected it was the future.

He had burned all the letters he had received from Wells, and he suddenly regretted that. He would write to him one more time, today.

9

As the month of July progressed, Marilyn's visions of the painter in her bedroom appeared more often. She imagined almost every night that the elderly painter with the unkempt beard had an easel in her bedroom, and he painted her portrait in the nude, in strokes that were sometimes slow, sometimes swift, always sure and accurate.

She awoke several times, hoping to find him at work at his easel, but he was never there. She came to believe that he was indeed actually in her bedroom, making her portrait, but that her act of awaking burst the bubble and made him disappear.

She knew that sounded crazy, but it seemed to make sense to her. She wanted to see the finished painting. He seemed to start it anew each evening, but never seemed able to finish it. She thought it was her fault. She came up with a plan. She would take enough barbiturates to keep her soundly asleep, so she wouldn't awake and he could finish the painting. She wouldn't even toss in her sleep. She'd be the perfect subject. And she'd awaken early in the morning, fully refreshed, and find the painting.

She decided not to tell her shrinks about her dreams of this painter, or her plan. As it was, they all thought she was crazy. She wanted to act again. She couldn't trust anyone -- they might be friends of friends of Darryl's.

No, she'd go this alone, and end up with a beautiful, shimmering watercolor portrait of her sleeping, and all the starring roles she could handle.

10

It was now August in England, and the last thing Wells needed in the heat was a fire. He wished his study had been equipped with one of those new residential air cooling units he had heard about from a friend in America. He still thought of England as the leader in scientific innovation in the world, but he knew that was no longer case, and hadn't been for several decades. Telephone, radio broadcasting, chemical air cooling all had begun across the Atlantic, in America, and were still barely available in England.

He wiped his brow with a lacy handkerchief, glared at the slowly moving overhead fan which was hardly doing its job, and turned to the manuscript at hand. He didn't really expect this to work in reality at all, but it was still a pretty good story. A famous painter contacts a famous writer of scientific fiction and says he wants to be able to paint a scene that has not happened, a scene in the future. The writer and the painter discuss the fine points of this for years, until the writer comes up with an idea: write a story in which this happens, a story in which the painter puts to canvas something that has not yet occurred, and if the spheres are properly aligned, this will actually happen.

But how would the writer know if this has happened? The writer would need proof -- which would be the painting.

***

Monet wasn't sure how many paintings he had left in him. He

wanted the painting of the blonde beauty to be just right, but so far that perfection had eluded him. He no longer saw her walking by the shore, but asleep in bed. He had several sketches of her in that pose, though what she was doing seemed real not a pose. On impulse, he burned all the paintings of her on the shore, and all the sketches of her in bed, just as he had done with some of his unsatisfactory lily paintings, years before. He wanted just one painting of her, the right painting.

She was a very difficult subject in his mind. Just when she was sound asleep, eyelids not quite covering her morning-blue eyes, she would awaken in his mind. She would move, much too quickly. He needed the subject of a masterpiece like this to be perfectly still. But the problem was he had no control over her -- she was after all not a willing model, but a figment in his mind. If Freud was right, he had far less control over what his mind served up to him than he might have wanted.

11

Marilyn's housekeeper Eunice was staying over this night. Marilyn didn't really want that -- who knew what impact it might have on the painter in her dreams, it might scare him away -- but she didn't have much of a choice. Although the woman was technically in Marilyn's employ, she had been hired by Marilyn at her shrink Greenspan's insistence, which meant that Marilyn more or less had to do whatever Eunice thought best about the house, including sleeping over if that's what Eunice wanted. The last thing Marilyn needed was Eunice reporting to Greenspan that Marilyn had been obstinate.

Marilyn was hoping for a breakthrough with the elderly painter tonight. She told Eunice not to disturb her -- she wanted a long, sound night's sleep.

"Of course," Eunice replied.

"Thank you," Marilyn said, annoyed at herself for being so grateful for this middle-aged drudge's agreement to her request. The woman was a writer, for God's sake, she should have more sensitivity to Marilyn's needs -- though Marilyn admitted to herself that she had never read a word of anything Eunice had written. She was also a decorator, though her talents, if she had them, had not been applied as yet to Marilyn's home.

Marilyn closed the door to her bedroom, took off her clothes, and carefully counted out the number of pills she wanted to swallow -- enough for a good night's sleep, with any luck, with no tossing and turning.   She took the pills and tucked herself in bed. She knew she couldn't will herself to dream, but hoped with all of her heart that her painter would appear and paint her in her entirety as she lay still and softy breathing in the sweet arms of Morpheus.

12

Monet looked out at his lilies in the afternoon, easel at hand. He began painting, and realized he was seeing far beyond the lilies. The petals parted in his mind, to reveal his beautiful model in slumber. He had started painting the lilies but realized he was painting the sleeper instead. Her curves were reminiscent of his lilies and their lines. And they moved gently back and forth with every breath she took, much like his lilies in a late day breeze. He wondered if her name was Lily -- no, her name didn't matter, her beauty surpassed any name.

The painting went surely and quickly. He marveled at it when it was finished. This one he wouldn't burn.

***

It was just a few days before Christmas, 1926. Wells was alone in his study. Jane was out on a last-minute shopping spree. There was a loud knock on his front door. No danger of this being the infamous Man from Porlock, who interrupted Coleridge's writing of "Xanadu," and sentenced it to forever being a beautiful beginning fragment of a poem. No, Wells had been working on nothing useful for almost a week now, obsessed with thinking he might be able to create a time travel of sorts just by thinking and writing about it. Indeed, he had actually written the little story to that effect, but had not yet decided how it should end.

The man at the door had a letter and a package. Wells thanked him, tipped him generously for Christmas, and opened the letter first.

Very bad and sad news. Claude Monet had died on the 5th of December. Cancer of the lung had taken his life, according to the editor at the French Mercury. His letter also spoke of what was in the package -- a final painting by Monet, which the painter had wanted Wells to have, to do with as he chose--

"Father," Anthony, his son, now 11, had come into the room. Wells had been so engrossed in the letter that he hadn't heard Anthony. Wells thought for a moment about Anthony's mother, Rebecca West, which Wells always did when he saw their son. She was a remarkable woman and a remarkable writer.

13

Anthony West looked at the copy of the *New York Mirror* on his desk in his summer home in Fisher's Island, New York. He had asked a friend at *The New Yorker* to send him copies of all these tabloids trumpeting the death of Marilyn Monroe, but the *Mirror* took the cake, and was a mirror indeed of the prurient interest that afflicted this world.

"Marilyn Monroe Kills Self," the front page proclaimed, in big, screaming letters, followed by "Found Nude in Bed ... Hand on Phone ... Took 40 Pills".

He supposed he should be glad that there wasn't a photo of Marilyn dead in the nude, though that would likely follow in rags even cheaper than the *Mirror*.

He had recognized Marilyn as soon as he had seen her in that John Huston movie, *Asphalt Jungle*, back in 1950, one of the very first he had seen in America. Her name was not even on the movie posters, but he had known who she was immediately -- the beautiful blonde, sound asleep and naked in bed, painted to watercolor perfection by his father's friend Claude Monet, shortly before the master Impressionist had died.

Anthony had been in the room when his father had unwrapped the package from France a few days before Christmas back in 1926. His father then told him the whole story, swore him to secrecy, and had entrusted the painting to him years later, right before he died, just after the Second World War.

The painting was just superb, but Anthony hadn't known what to make of it or the story that accompanied it, and seeing Marilyn Monroe on the screen for the first time in 1950 had only shown a partial light on this mystery.

How had a painter who died in 1926 painted a portrait of an actress who wouldn't become famous until three decades later? There was some connection between the two, for sure -- a cosmic connection of some sort. Marilyn Monroe had been born in 1926, the year in which Monet had died in December.

Anthony had seen every other movie with the stunning star after *The Asphalt Jungle*. He had toyed with contacting her, showing her the portrait, but she'd never believe his story, not for an instant. She'd assume that the painting had been done by a Monet forger, after Marilyn had become world-renown and long after Monet had died.

But Anthony knew better. He had been there in that room, shortly after the package with the painting had arrived in his father's study in 1926.

And he had indeed told no one at all about this. Now that Marilyn Monroe was dead, perhaps he would write something about this for *The New Yorker*. His father had never shared the unfinished story he had been writing about this -- the story that was supposed to make this all come true in the future -- and Anthony had been unable to find a copy of it in his father's effects. The premise of the story seemed much more out of this world than his father's other fiction -- insane, frankly -- but he had learned to put nothing past his beloved old man.

Anthony sighed. Maybe his father had given an only copy of the story to someone else, one of his lovers, or their offspring.

He went to the closet where he kept the painting, carefully wrapped so it looked like nothing special. He hadn't looked at it in a few months.

No one was home. He carefully unwrapped it and looked at it now. It could almost have been a portrait of Marilyn in death, as she was now, except Monet had imbued it with a subtle but unmistakable energy which spoke of her alive -- deeply asleep, to be sure, but alive. Monet had the talent to show that.

There was more mystery here than even Anthony West, with all that he knew, was able to fathom. He didn't know if he ever would.

He heard his front door open downstairs. That would be his sweet wife, Lily. He carefully rewrapped the painting, put it back, deep in the closet, and went downstairs to greet her.

Yes, there were deeper connections here, too far under the surface for him to see, certainly today. He would decide what to do about this extraordinary painting across time some other day.

###

ABOUT THE AUTHOR

Paul Levinson, PhD, is Professor of Communication & Media Studies at Fordham University in NYC. His nonfiction books, including *The Soft Edge* (1997), *Digital McLuhan* (1999), *Realspace* (2003), *Cellphone* (2004), and *New New Media* (2009; 2nd edition, 2012), have been translated into fifteen languages. His science fiction novels include *The Silk Code* (winner of Locus Award for Best First Science Fiction Novel of 1999), *Borrowed Tides* (2001), *The Consciousness Plague* (2002), *The Pixel Eye* (2003), *The Plot To Save Socrates* (2006), *Unburning Alexandria* (2013), *Chronica* (2014), and *It's Real Life: An Alternate History of The Beatles* (2024). His novelette, "The Chronology Protection Case," was made into a short movie available on Amazon Prime. His alternate history short story about The Beatles, "It's Real Life," was made into a radio play, won The Mary Shelley Award for Outstanding Fiction, and was expanded into a novel *It's Real Life: An Alternate History of The Beatles* published in 2024. His novelette, "Robinson Calculator," was published in the *Robots Through the Ages* anthology in July 2023. He was President of the Science Fiction Writers of America (SFWA) 1998-2001. He has appeared on CNN, MSNBC, Fox News, the Discovery Channel, National Geographic, the History Channel, NPR, and numerous TV and radio programs. His 1972 LP, *Twice Upon a Rhyme*, was re-issued in 2010. His first LP since 1972, *Welcome Up: Songs of Space and Time*, was released in 2020 by Old Bear Records and Light in the Attic Records.

BOOKS BY PAUL LEVINSON

The following books by Paul Levinson are available on Kindle and paperback:

Science fiction:

It's Real Life: An Alternate History of The Beatles

Loose Ends (time travel) series (complete):
Loose Ends, Little Differences, Late Lessons, Last Calls; or, all four in The Loose Ends Saga

Sierra Waters (time travel) series:
The Plot to Save Socrates, Unburning Alexandria, Chronica

Phil D'Amato forensic detective series:
The Chronology Protection Case,The Copyright Notice Case, The Silk Code, The Consciousness Plague, The Pixel Eye

Ian's Ions and Eons (three time travel novelettes)

Exo-Genetic Engineers series
The Orchard, The Suspended Fourth

Double Realities series
The Other Car, Extra Credit, The Wallet, The P&A

Borrowed Tides

The Kid in the Video Store

Peter Brown Called: Tales of SciFi and Music

Urban Corridors: Fables and Gables

Robinson Calculator

Nonfiction and Science Fiction

Touching the Face of the Cosmos: On the Intersection of Space Travel and Religion
an anthology of essays and science fiction stories, including the final interview with John Glenn, an essay by Guy Consolmagno, SJ (the "Pope's Astronomer"), and contributions from leading thinkers about the role of religion in space travel

Nonfiction:

The Soft Edge: A Natural History and Future of the Information Revolution

Digital McLuhan: A Guide to the Information Millennium

Realspace: The Fate of Physical Presence in the Digital Age, On and Off Planet

New New Media

From Media Theory to Space Odyssey: Petar Jandrić interviews Paul Levinson

Fake News in Real Context

Cyber War and Peace

Human Replay: A Theory of the Evolution of Media, original PhD dissertation, 1979, New York University.

www.ingramcontent.com/pod-product-compliance
Lightning Source LLC
Chambersburg PA
CBHW021959190626
46808CB00017B/3041